WHILE THE MORNING STARS SANG TOGETHER

JJ BRINSKI

WHILE>>>>>>>

THE>>>>>>

MORNING>>>

STARS>>>>

SANG>>>>>>

TOGETHER>>>>

>>>>>>>>>>>>>>>>>>>>jj brinski

WHILE THE MORNING STARS SANG TOGETHER

First Edition printed in March, 2024

ISBN: 979-8-9899789-0-8

Cover art Jamin Still, acrylic on black canvas panel.
Formatting by Andrea Renae.

Much of my work can be viewed on Instagram under the handle @jjbrinski

Why? Websites take forever to build.

TABLE OF CONTENTS

INTRO

POETRY & STORIES

OUTRO

The Hubble and Webb telescopes have caused us to recognize better than any other generation how we lack a frame of reference for properly conceiving of most of the matter that exists. In the way that good Art does, JJ Brinski simultaneously pacifies and intensifies the anxiety that that creates. WHILE THE MORNING STARS SANG TOGETHER heaves with the beyond-matter of the possibility of language. It too, stimulates the growth of courage that trust in what is wholly Other but found near, requires.

—Corey Frey, just another bearded fella: multi-disciplinary artist, poet, and art educator. Fellow Maker & Mystic.

Approach these poems with the knowledge that nothing exists quite like them. JJ is an image bearer, a creature created to create, who's cracked open the seams of the universe above with these life-giving words. A brave astronaut exploring galaxies, he's brought us slivers of planets he's landed upon. These poems are worth all the effort it took to inscribe them onto paper. If you squint your eyes, the stardust still shimmers in their curves.

—**Rachael Watson, fiction writer, restless creative, life-long sci-fi enthusiast.**

Brinski's collection takes the reader to an entirely new plane of the poetic cosmos. If you have not yet encountered science fiction space poetry, you'll never forget this introduction. Brinski makes the space theme his own, with boldness and reverence and vision. This collection is playful, pensive, musical. But mostly, it is worshipful. He lauds the Creator—known in this collection by such rich names as Starspitter and Suncrafter—with burning words that land on the page as pure praise.

—**Vanessa Howard, writer, author with Twenty Hills, Quill & Flame, Nightshade ... puts the magic in Flash Fiction Magic!**

WHILE THE MORNING STARS SANG TOGETHER is an unconventional collection of poetry and short fiction from poet JJ Brinski. Lovers of science fiction and verse brimming with honesty and depth will find themselves coming back to this collection again and again. Brinski writes within the realm of the Starspitter, a science fiction allegory of the Creator. It is honest and deeply personal. It takes the reader into the emotional lives of the characters but also the author himself, leading the reader to see and understand that in their hardest places, they are not alone. Oftentimes poetry is collected in such a fashion that the reader can simply pick up a book and choose a poem at random. Readers are definitely welcome to do that, and it works just fine. However, Brinski orders these poems as if they were a carefully curated playlist, and the flow from piece to piece tells a deeper story that packs a punch. If you are a lover of science fiction, poetry, or even just someone who loves a collection that is a little out of the ordinary, I highly recommend picking up this work.

—Kelly Hellmuth, Havok-published author, Flash Fiction Magician, hella teacher.

Buckle up and prepare to have your "retinas wrecked" — JJ Brinski's latest collection of poems and flash fiction is a must-read, wild, beautiful ride that invites you to stop and smell the cosmos. WHILE THE MORNING STARS SANG TOGETHER teaches us, verse by verse, to wonder at both the impossibly infinite and impossibly minute nature of the universe and, finally, the impossibly loving nature of the One who created it all.

—Sarah Spradlin, fellow Rabbit Room poet and co-host of the Poetry Pub Open Mic, farmer in Nicaragua.

To anyone who has ever heard the stars speak...

or sing:

this collection is for you.

INTRODUCTION>>>>>>>>>>>>

Somewhere between seeing *Return of the Jedi*, watching *E.T.* in the front row of the Strand Theatre in Crawfordsville, IN, and being frozen in terror and awe when *Close Encounters of the Third Kind* was playing on TV at like six years old, I became enthralled, fascinated, shimmer-dipped in wonder through science fiction and space stories. Later, a VHS tape pirated from cable TV was shown to me with a couple fast-forwarded scenes likely containing a bit of bare she-flesh. The title of that nail-biting, heart-thumping, futuristic death parade was *The Terminator*. I was smitten, imprinted, stamped by machines, enamored by fights for humanity and existence, curious about aliens and other worlds, and if we could ever, ever get there—and how.

Even later, I grabbed a copy of Ridley Scott's director's cut of the seminal cosmic horror *Alien* and immediately had to write a poem about it my freshman year of college. As far as I can remember, that may have been the very first time I married my love for creative writing and poetry—stemming from a wonderfully flame-fanning ninth-grade English teacher—with the swimming stars and vivid vastitude of both the near and far reaches of what we broadly, lumpingly call "space." A few years later, in my last year of college, I had the grand opportunity of having my first poem published through my university creative writing and arts journal named *The Aerie*. The poem that was selected was a little piece called *...And the Stars Were Born*. This was a playful, cosmic, somewhat folkloric glimpse of a Speaker voicing the stars as sounds and syllables, hurling them into existence as words mouthed. And there you have it, my venture into this spacious comet ride of sci-fi poetry pondering far-flung largeness rode out into the wide universe as a satellite shot from Earth to photograph and observe everything it would see. With a poem on starbirth, my own cluster of space and sci-fi poetry began.

And now, well, I have just been fueling the forge, stoking it to superheated temps. Throw in bottles full of Lewis' *Out of the Silent Planet, Perelandra,* and *That Hideous Strength*. Toss in the mythology of the opening chapters of *The Silmarillion*. Add in *Hitchhiker's Guide to the Galaxy* and *The Guardians of the Galaxy* for levity and playful language, laughing as I skip amongst the constellations. *The Expanse* series taught me intricacies of near-space/system politics and possibilities of terraforming, and witty space cowboys were sprinkled in from *Firefly*. There are so many more dashes of color and spark from the original writings of Pierre Boule (*Planet of the Apes*) and H.G. Wells (especially *War of the Worlds*) and more contemporary additions like *The Left Hand of Darkness* (Ursula K. LeGuin), EVERYTHING by Ray Bradbury—including his obscure poetry—and even some Orson Scott Card.

All in all, with this collection of space and sci-fi poems and quirky flash-fiction stories (some from a larger story universe called the "Spitterverse"), I am finally able to be the explorer I've always wanted to be. Pressing forward into the expanse, the near limitlessness of the trillions and trillions of suns and the new exoplanets they discover almost every day, I find myself able to go pretty much anywhere my mind can conceive, touching down only long enough to collect food stores, supplies, and new James Webb data, only to launch into galaxies and worlds far away and even some far, far away. My hope is that you will learn to run into the overabundance of wonder, fly into multitudinous beauty, experiencing the transporting sensation of what C.S. always referred to as the "more and not less" of the Divine. It was also Lewis who flipped the space travel tropes on their heads by introducing the idea that maybe space and "the beyond" could contain warmth and teeming life, and not just the cold void of fear and darkness. To that end and to all of these travelers, wonderers, storytellers, works and worlds, I am forever grateful.

Without further ado, let me take you to space....

JJ Brinski, the Mad Space Poet,
November 2023

HOW TO READ THIS BOOK

A word on pacing:

In a word, slow. Try to read this book slow. Take a couple or a few poems at a time. Or, if you just have to read fast, take it slower the second time through (wink). And just so we're clear, I would never want to be so pretentious as to ask that you only take your time with my poetry and stories in this collection. Poetry and distilled pieces, in general, should be read at a different pace because each word is—hopefully—worth four or five or 187 elsewhere. But, yeah, take your time; the machines already have us doing everything else too fast. Maybe this is how we beat them. To help, guess what? I wrote another poem and I thought it might just come in handy here:

Look, I Know Poetry is Hard to Read...

Take poetry in sips
like fine, florid drink.
Swirl it around
in mouth and mind.
Chew it like tender meat or morsel,
let every bit of its flavor
and flare collide, coalescing
with every taste budding.
Work it around, with tongue
used for telling and talk.
Make. Those. Sounds.
with.....................................
Breath. Movement. Thought.
Back & forth, forward & behind,
swallow with savor and sigh.
May this wad of words
be sweet sustaining
to your gaping, hunger-sown soul.

"Astronomy compels
the soul
to look upward
and leads us from
this world
to another."

—Plato.

"Astronomy compels
the soul
to look upward
and leads us from
this world
to another."

—Plato.

EX_PANDER

Crack the cosmos.
Pour out of starrish mist. Explode
through all the vapors
and colors of glory,
the death and rebirth of suns,
the spinning of spheres....
Oh greet me in the morning
with galaxies in your eyes.
Maker of vast collections,
of holy displays,
of fluorescent viewscapes.
Oh wreck my retinas for beauty!
Oh clobber me whole!
Cleave my mind afresh;
pour in your platinum,
liquified jewels,
solder with silver seam,
glue with goldlode,
open up this head
like a comet-carved cloud canyon
and fill. Overflow. Expand,
oh Expander of Worlds.

WITH ONE LOOK AT
THE ORION NEBULA

This stellar nursery.
This violet place of star tissue,
the closest womanly womb in the cosmos.
With watercolor hues of
hydrogen, oxygen and sulfur,
folds of slight azure, soft purplish indigo,
and lovely lavender cloud smoke.
I hear you are most visible
with our naked eyes inside our Januaries.
I hear you are the nearest of your kind,
yet I cannot stretch my mind to
the lightyear's length.
I also hear that you have a sun-studded belt
that only the fashioning hands of Yahweh,
Archbuilder of Astro-regions,
can loosen.

DEEP SPACE
IN TWO MOVEMENTS

<<<<MOVEMENT 1>>>>

You cut caverns
in far-off quartz,
on surfaces alien
and unseen.
You set the span
of the lightyear's
luminous length.

<<<<<MOVEMENT 2>>>>>

You speak
and planets know
how to spin & tilt,
proper for life or
atmosphere. You breathe
gasses in admixture,
so as not to explode.

You perform these feats in
far reaches, needing no
mortal eyes to validate.

UNMANNED

"It's so quiet," he thought internally
or maybe said in a sub-whisper—
he could not quite tell the difference.
"I guess space has no soundtrack
save the loop of words spinning,
flashing in your head."
Star stuff streaked by his slow craft drifting,
no sphaera in sight out here,
passing beyond the Arc of Nine.

"The end of all star clouds is shatteringly silent,
but a symphony for the eyes."
He took a breath. No fog on glass.
Ahead of his thoughts, way out here,
the swirlish curling of stars occurs,
towering up like a light-speckled wave
that would never crash—suspended.

"I bet they would have music for this,
a soundtrack, a poetry," digital images
of his programmers shot up
on the cockpit glass.
His gears and wires warmed,
his CPU whirred with life.

Images were sent home.

<u>WING HAS OVERCOME WIRE</u>

or Crowen Kestrellen Has Claimed His Throne

All hail! All hail!!
Throne and crown are established,
for wing has overcome wire!

What is the sound of layered
aluminum alloy under talons sharp
and knife-edge thin?
What scraping tones ring from
the wretched cyborgian usurpers'
ugly-angled and mangled
metal bodies, these
less-than-halfbreeds having
magnesium skulls
we individually lit to explode?

What is the pounding thrum that
percussively approaches?
Clawfoot stomp, butt end spear,
clawfoot stomp, butt end spear.

Stop. Double tap. Double-rank.
Steel spears clash, clank...
forming a tunnel of honor,
a thoroughfare of
regality, reward
as many pinioned men of
warrish wing-wound stood
on yonder right, and yonder left.

All hail! All hail!!
Throne and crown are established,
for wing has overcome wire!

What aisle now fills with the song
of the kill-shot velocities,
the virile victories,
the chanting conquerors
over riveted shells
unriveted by force, stomped into
coal-black moon dust,
where no breath breathes
within their crack-riddled,
carbon fiber ribs?

What was the titanic
cataclysm-metallic, cephalic

carnage and collapse...
ringing of slicing wire and
severed feather?
We, eagle-angelic,
defending lung and
bone, eye and beak.
They, twisted frames
of world-scourging limbs
abysmal, humanoids weaponized
by advanced bionic brains
hive-held and bound, brutal
facsimile men-of-metal
heart and tissue corroded,
yea, even compromised.

All hail! All hail!!
Throne and crown are established,
for wing has overcome wire!

What are these sounds: the rising
to taloned feet, the scraping,
the pounding, the song—these
echoes of galaxy-wide conflict
of ripped wing and crushed skulls
cybernetic?

This, oh Legend Scrawler, let the
scrolls forever glow with starlight
luster, this...
is the sound of the
Warrior King Crowen Kestrellen
coming to his feet above
a newly fashioned throne
of cyborg chassis,
carcass-conglomerate.
Atop his silvery, plumed brow
shimmers a twisted circlet
of wire, wrapped circuitry, coiled cable,
the mayhemic metal innards
torn from their wasted, wrecked
warlord. Out of his corpse, a crown.

...and a hush fell over the
once-heaving heavens.

All hail! All hail!!
Throne and crown are established
for wing has overcome wire!

MIDDLEMEN OF THE LATE-WANED EARTH

The middle is where we all live.
One foot in this world, the other,
in another.
On this Earth there is a braided tension.
It flows like an ether down veinish trails
destined for our forgiven footfalls.
This liquid nerve, this volatile ribbon taut,
throbs in the going of our way.
Middlemen of a late-waned planet,
threading light and dark spaces on their way
to a celestially-saturated terrestrial remake.
Come now stars and wing'ed ones!
Come now fall, come thou reprise!
It's all about to snap...
with the empyrean orchestra poised,
clutching instruments of symphonies
rapturous and New.

FIREBRAIN, BURN

Firebrain, burn.

Organize, set up
in rows, inside the cerebrum,
sparked by thinking's throes.
Sequence and saintliness,
new things to behold,
to rise up, burst, and
illuminate the old.
Sweet neurotheology,
blessed brain-bound biology,
anointed and dripping
with holy honey,
branching forth
to thoughts and
thunderings lit,
to further spinnings
yet unspun or split.

Firebrain, burn.

OF GRAVEL & GRANDEUR

Dirt and decibels, driven at launch,
Roots and rockets,
Lightyears and loam,
Thrusters and thrushes,
Birds and binary code...
Droids and dust kicked-up.

Farmers and physicists,
Pilots and plows.
Foraging, terraforming,
War machines, and windmills.
Gasoline powered or nuclear fusion?
Country roads or space lanes?

Circuits and cicadas,
Lasers and locusts.
Androids and ants,
Bees and metal bees, with cameras for eyes.
Dronebuzz drones, squawking hawks.
Termites and Terminators.

Tank-mech tracks and traveled trails,
Cyborgs and sunsets,
Antlers and animatronics,
Horns and hovercrafts.
Black holes, black soil,
Firmed earth, fountains of atmosphere.

Solar storms, rain and thunder,
Alien life, dogs and cats.
Burly beards, scintillating scales,
Soft skin and slimy secretions.
Talking words, shrieking shrieks.
Liquid metal, running rivers and creeks.

Earth and every opus,
in mind and in space,
microscopic, macro in scope,
here and on planets trillionfold,
the Starspeaker, Earthwhirler,
originates alone, matchless
in vastitudinous aptitude,
skilled beyond skill.

COSMOS IN SKULL &
THE GOD OF SPACE

*a maker's prayer, set to the tune of Hammock's
Sleepover Series, Vol. 2*

Father of Flashing Lights,
thank you for robots and androids,
every imaginary and living thing,
creation and sub-creation....
Oh God of beeps and boops,
space travel and alien craft,
lo, you are Master of
begotten and dying stars,
how mighty art Thou,
cupping all things colossal.
And in the aerospace avenues of the mind,
let all thought and dream and
sound and hush, all curve and angle,

all rising up, all lying down—
everything thought up by me
and everything thought up by you—
be motions, sweet mechanizations
to compute your great grace and
infinitude, inside one,
slightly problematic
skull of man—imperfect,
limited, anointed.

LEATHER SKELETON

Structural, slightly flexible, but shape,
it holds. Durable, but must be broken
in, again. Flexible, but not much at first.
Orthodox rigidity meets well-tooled give,
but ya gotta break it in
with oil, sweat, and use.
The roughing up causes
a less-textured relax...
of surface, coarse feature.
Yes, it's weird that friction
makes things smooth,
especially when it's your skeleton,
and it lives on the inside.

thoughts

Racing. Lights on wires worn,
new wires too, of copper, brass...
a couple titanium, vibrate,
sizzle. Thoughts like
slow lightning form, crack off like
breaking glass in flat plainlike panes.
The surface is moving, removing, it
gets moving 8,300 times a dammed day...
like water held back, then let loose,
producing a million watts.
A MILLION BOUNDLESS, BRILLIANT WATTS!
Electricity. Racing. Lacing
the brain like lasers,
but all-together untraceable,
untrailable, untrainable.
Or are they?

THE SHELF LIFE OF WORDS

1.
Sometimes you come back to your words
and they all look slimy sad,
sideways, slipshod. Like,
they fell over and slid out of a rusted
lid, barely holding to the threads of an old
jar you should have never ever put them in.
There is life in them still. See how they
gasp for air outside this
ill-fitting confinement.
They need to be read.
They need a good sounding.

2.
The shelflife effect. Stored, maybe
incarcerated thoughtlessly,
these warm-blooded words
gurgle and sputter to be let out...
like a clone,
left in fluids,
in that thick glass cylinder,
on a bygone planet...
just dying to breathe.

THE_WOES_OF_SPACE_ TRAVEL

If you ever leave an ashen, old Earth
with all exploratory fanfare,
furthering a humanly hope,
and you get to Mars
or somehow settle on one
of Saturn's moons...
you may soon see that
what you left,
what you sought decidedly to decamp,
smuggled itself within the
compartments of your exoskeleton.
Genetics. DNA. The cellular you.
You brought the bad.
You brought it here.
There is no spacial escape.
It will leap from you.
It will scurry, slither, and kill
and you better learn to deal.

>>>>>>>>>

>>>>>>>

>>>>OH>>>>>>>>

>>>>>THE

>>>WOES>>>

>>>>>>OF

SPACE>>>>>>

>>>TRAVEL

>>>>>>

>>>>>>>>>>>>

THE TINIEST ASTRONAUT

Loretta-Louise Powers was the tiniest astronaut ever fired into space, unbeknownst to nearly everyone on Earth. When someone is less than an eighth of an inch tall, strapped to two full-sized oxygen tanks inside a life pod not much bigger than an Altoids tin, it is very easy to go unnoticed.

After she shrunk herself in a bad engineering experiment at MIT, her job prospects were a bit slim. To make things worse, they brought her to NASA in a quite poorly-furnished matchbox, which is always insulting for a PhD. And somehow, the four TOP SECRET, high-clearance bozos who ran the spacecraft program were able to talk Loretta-Louise into it, after a quarter thimble of whiskey of course.

But now, Dr. Shotzke had died in a car accident, Captain Carlson disappeared after retirement, Halle Hetty got a job in Hollywood, and the last one monitoring her communications was suffering from dementia, as far as she could tell, and hadn't responded to her in two years, four months, and 13 days. "Thanks for nothing Gilbert!"

Several years back, she had left the solar system—full interstellar. She had been closer to Jupiter, Saturn, Neptune, and Uranus *cough* than any living soul, and no one knew. She had eaten a record-breaking amount of dehydrated micro-food, slurped more Tang than a full-sized seven-year-old, and all this without one TV appearance involving squeeze cheese floating in zero gravity or an embarrassing explanation of recycling her own urine. But the things her tiny eyes had seen through that two-by-two inch viewing window! Vast. Alien. Stellar landscapes and streaks of light to melt the mind and reform it into praise for its origin.

It was now just before her 70th birthday, in radio silence, and Loretta-Louise was sick to death of the eighteen shrunken books she had and the stupid-tiny card deck for solitaire she'd almost worn blank, but instead of feeling further from everything, she felt closer—to something.

And maybe someday, someone would find her star

logs and observations as backtracks on the Voyager's radio messages and she'd get a small-town, Midwestern gym named after her.

NOISE • MACHINE

I felt the pressure and thrust today
of machines and their men
whirling about and stuffing my peace
with noise. They sang a dissonant chorus,
"Why don't you move and
go and get things done?!"
These noisemakers with their voxes
want to run me into the ground. Their drums
of "Progress!" quickened and grew louder.
And all I wanted was to breathe
and watch my chest heave unhindered,
and Christly free. Away with all the busy-
busy, go-go hustle crap!
Work to live it up,
work so hard you die trying.
No thanks.

Give me a book and a backyard
and children running, laughing,
and cell phones far away.
Kill the linked machines; they never stop
beeping and notifying and calling to you,
"Oh dopamine! Oh online persona!"

    Give me a break...
    give me a clean break...
break me off a piece of that
slowdown-quiet...
shut-your-mouth...
capture leisurely breath...

exhale calm.

OUR BLESSED DROIDSMITH

Oh my Lord, you dismantle me,
so do it delicately...
like a dysfunctional droid,
a machine you love with glad grace.
Tenderly, remove from me this
shield and shell, plates and layers,
leg joints and arm joints, all metal
on metal, cable and socket.
Unrivet me slow, oh my Mechanic
with steady hands.
Oh thou Tinkerer, Droidsmith,
holding all instruments
of creation in your ornate toolbox...
here lies the mangled me, a wad of
wires and plugs, motors and servos.

Master of Living Robotics,
you know how I work and whirl,
how I move on my mounts and pivots.
Dismantle me, so delicately.
I promise half of me won't try to
drag itself off the workbench again.
I will hold back my words,
but I will look you in the eye
while you work and weep an oil
of engines and joys,
movements and stillnesses.
Please gaze back at me
with a smile full of upshifting
upgrades and trusted tweaks.
Let these warm wires with soul…
worship you for the handling.

For you dismantle me,
ever-so delicately.

"Again I will
build you
so that you
will be
rebuilt...."
—Jeremiah 31:4

DROID'S FIRST DREAM

It is no secret that Droidanians never really wake up. This is probably because they never really sleep. Their AI is advanced, brainlike, and incredibly fast-thinking, but when it's on, it's on... and when it's off, it's...just off. Z(9) was never shut down because he had the cold and lonely task of piloting the "Tozer Bull" while the rest of the crew took an eight-month space nap.

While en route to explore the neighboring system, Z(9) had monitored the ship's flight path, the crew's heartbeats and vital organ function, and even administered liquid sustenance through food tubes. But the most exciting job he had was monitoring the elevated neuro-activity of the crew as they dreamed and told jumbled tales to themselves made up of experiences and highlights of life, shoving through whimsical, playful, or unrealistically terrifying storyscapes. Internal, surrealistic visuals. Stupefying creatures. Ridiculous relationships. Public functions and school classes, sans pants. Wild and wonderful...and Z(9) began to be curious of what jealousy meant.

Droidanians were lifelike, quick problem solvers, always won at strategy games, had more factoids than anyone ever wanted to hear. But, they could never go on stupid-wild adventures in deep sleep. He couldn't dream and he knew it. He didn't know what happened when he was "switched off" except for probably some invasive metal tool prodding, the downloading of data, and slumped, unpuppeteered corner-leaning. It sounded like a bad joke, a stab in the chest cavity.... And now Z(9) started to feel the heat of enmeshed circuits that could only be described as simulated, learning-but-childish, anger.

It left shortly after it arrived in his mind...and he relaxed. More important duties were at hand. It was time to start the two-day process of waking the crew. Sealed pods unsealed. Heartbeat monitors sped up and slowed down. Breathy fog coated the convex glass in front of each face. Five of them to be exact. Z(9) was accomplished and purposeful again. He helped take the feeding tubes out. He held the puke buckets. He checked pupils and skin tone and muscle elasticity and got everybody up and running so they could finally shut him down for a couple days.

Z(9) needed a full diagnostic, and the crew needed his intel and data from the last eight months. "Time for a nice break, Z...a little neuro-net snooze." Doctor Sheeg flipped his shutdown switch.

"An untimely jab, to be sure," Z thought and started to mutter. "I do wish I could dream like I saw you all doing Doctor...so carefree and wonder-filled. Wouldn't...that...be...."

His words slowed at the end of his out-speaking thoughts as Sheeg began the download phase. Z(9) was out and offline for the next 48 hours.

"I really wish I could make you dream buddy, but that's just not how it works."

[His AI went down. Full darkness. No input.]

Z(9) woke. "You did it Doctor! I don't know how... an upgrade...a new backup system link to pre-stored dream sequences.... But really, you did it!

Thank you so very much!"

"You did...what exactly?" said the Captain, shuffling slowly over, his trusty USSEC Tozer Bull mug in his hand, steaming with cobalt coffee.

Sheeg shrugged a flummoxed kinda shrug.

"Well, sir, I dreamed for the first time...at least I think I did. You were there quietly piloting through fountains of sweat...and Bashan's fur was on fire at one point, his shoulder fur." Z(9) turned and gestured toward the hulking Yettish alien, "Your right shoulder—full flames!"

"Redge was inventing new profanities amidst the creature-danger, Dr. Sheeg was dissecting some charred, unidentifiable 'remains'...and Fleeda got sucked out the forward airlock! Uh, she seemed to be on a safety tether, of course. At least I think she was?" Z(9) rubbed his chin in ponderful amusement at his dreamlike recollections. He had seen professors do this in historical videos.

Fleeda folded her pissed-off arms trying to remember how droid dismemberment worked.

Everyone else looked at each other dumbstruck of tongue and befuddled.

"Oh, and there was much flying, and yelling...and chasing, come to think of it. We were dodging debris, searching manically for something—I can't quite remember—there were dark, winged things pursuing us for what felt like hours—although my timeline is admittedly difficult to calculate—implosions, ruins, runes, messages. It was exhilarating! It was...."

He faded off, scanning the dumbfounded, unsettling looks on the crew's faces. "Yes, and let there be no mistake about this fact, we were in considerable danger."

Lessons on fear and horrified surprise were now added to his databank.

(a jealousy of angels)

Have not **I**
gazed on to **see**
space beyond **the**
spaces where I dwell, **stars**
strewn, nebulas swirling. **I**
think only of astro-angels. I **hear**
them bragging and telling tales, **the**
sailors on black seas swagger, **rolling**
through galaxies, where supernovas **thunder**.

I>>>>>

SEE>>>

THE STARS>>

I>>>>>>>>

HEAR>>>>>

THE>>>>

ROLLING>>>>>

THUNDER>>>>>>

IT WAS STAR WARS

I really think it was Star Wars...
Return of the Jedi...
in the Strand Theater,
at age six with my dad, to be exact,
and later wearing out the whole trilogy
on VHS with my brother Matthew.
Then light-speeding through stretching stars,
zipping in the Falcon
from Tatooine to Hoth.
Laser swords and alien races:
some furry, some Wookiee, some
lizard wearing yellow (Bossk),
some green wearing orange (Greedo).
Everything far, far away
in a galaxy, a broad universe
big enough for my imagination.
I'm sure of it now.
It was Han in his space-freighter
and his friendship with Luke,
it was a Skywalker story,
a religion of Jedi space heroes
that baptized me into sci-fi,
and gave birth to starwonder.

LUMINOUS BEINGS ARE WE

—Master Yoda

A HOPE BEYOND THE MOON EUROPA

Out the fog-frosted panes
this morning,
the pulse of the year
had slowed, lessened.
Sugar softness now covered
the all-too-familiar
and I too relaxed, down-shifted,
with clean breaths and
honest sighs of glad tidings.
It was the first real snow;
it smelled like water laying still...
it announced its arrival by
eating the Earth's echoes.
and the *liturgy tells me this
is a fresh canvas, a do-over.

I hope beyond the moon Europa
that this is true.

*Doug McKelvey, "A Liturgy for the First Snow"
from *Every Moment Holy Vol. 1*

HIMNARÌKI

In the highest of highness,
in the furthest of fires.
The genesis of light...
the womb of starbirth...
the zenith of Mind...
the beginning of brainburst.
THIS...this is where you reside.
On a throne of nebula, varicolored,
suns in their surrounds
make for your pavement.
(for you are above, always above)

Dark matter and black holes bow.
Quasars and pulsars ignite your crown.
Neutron stars and supergiants,
white dwarves and massives
all revel at their given names
and praise you with rousing
resplendence.

"Lord of Light, searing and supreme...
You alone are Starspitter,
undiminished and true."

ALL THE BOOKS

(a commentary)

"...I suppose not even the world itself could contain the books that would be written." —John 21:25

Think of all the books, written through all the ages. Stories, fictional and non. Poems. Biographies. Histories. Books full of lyric and song, horror and triumph. Now think about God as Author-Perfect, and we his poíēma, such intricate little verses. Let your mind and heart peel back like pages. You are a spacious story inlaid with spirit. Your life, a beatified, bound book in scribal hands. His pen has pricked your skin for truth; his ink has healed your blood. You are glowing words etched, crimson calligraphy. You are word and you are art. You are meant for the living libraries of the New Creation. Your pages will decorate the third heaven. There, we who have been written will write forevermore.

Books, fill up the world!
If all stories are written...
in the New, they will.

GOING DARK

I will go dark,
retreat for a bit
to retrieve light,
to gather it like
choice, glowing fruit.
And I'll bring
some back for you,
my friends.

dROPS

And I saw, as it were, through orange-gold rainclouds, a surface below, dry and strewn with rock. I had heard it was once verdant and lush, long ago when branching giants roamed the sphaera. It was an average summer day on Itse Hillintä that we fell, headfirst like cool comets, but we hadn't fallen in many arcs, my brothers and I— not here. Beyond the higher clouds, stars winked through; at our backs, praising us, urging us on. But down was ground. And so, we let go of our mothering, nimbostratus homes—700 quadrillion of us.

This was no race, but we fell fast, the largest of us first. Liquid glared as horizontal setting sunlight cracked and cut through the lot of us, and I grinned through no mouth at all. We looked pretty boss, shooting like screaming streamers high in the atmosphere with singular purpose and galvanized unity.

Again, this was no race, but race down we did, for speed and swollen meaning. Down, down, down, we dropped towards the thirsty mouth of a sphaera gone dry: sorely, pitifully, to-the-very-brink ARID. So we felt that unweighted burden of intent and design and all the things we good elementals love to feel. That surface needed us. It beckoned us to transform, to calm, to soften, to break up, to penetrate, to build, to enliven where all was almost lost. We, I tell you, were emissaries of the Starspitter, himself...yet here, he became the Cloudking, the Sprayer of Life, the Restorer of Fields to Plow In.

Further and faster we fell as a sweet-soaked swarm, a rushing, fertile, virile army paratrooping with no chutes, no brakes, no hurry, but no patience either. Even...faster...we...fell.

And before we hit terminal velocity, the grand reason stamped behind unopening eyelids was read clear by us all. The ultimate purpose. The gorgeous calling forth: to speed and speed, flashing to the ground and hit it as hard as we could possibly hit, aerating, piercing it through like volleyed bullets and darts. You see, we were sent to seek seed, my brothers and sisters and me—maybe the last offspring of the great trees. To splash and flow through grit, grime, sand, and soil. To locate the last of the aeons-dormant, husked life...to knock on its door, to wake it up. A kiss from the Spitter himself. A calling forth from tomb. A wetted waking.

We struck. We watered. We flowed, pooled, seeped, and waited. The confined kernel had been dry, parched, lying in death so long, til I alone crashed against its ancient gates, its everlasting doors, closed since the First Aeon, now open to my trailing siblings. I splashed my watery arms as hard as I could splash; I struck hard and true. My one shot pierced the veil. My mission complete; I dripped away and died....

I droplet. I rain. I, waker of Trunklords. Herald to branch and leaf, waterspeaker to voice and limb.

*The Starspitter: the undiminished and true, god or deity.
*Itse Hillintä: one of the eight planets of the Arc of Nine galaxy.
*Trunklords: sentient tree-like creatures.

I PLAN TO LIVE FOREVER

permanence
    transcends
        endings.
            numinous
                feet
                    will keep
                        traipsing
                        through
                all barriers
              and beyonds,
        as soil
      and star
    are reborn,
under and above.

VERSION U.POINT.0

You are the only you,
hand-crafted,
stitched and knit,
a sui generis design.
You are
full-spec version U.0
stamped by your Maker
with his seal, his image,
his pre-computer hard-wiring.
A Creator created.
A Fleshbuilder built.

No star is the same
no planet a double,
no sunrise or sunset,
no person an exact copy of
another.
(clones are not his business)
A soul you have to drive you,
a spirit to ponder the cosmos
and reach for the holy hem of God,
through light beam and kindness.
Through cross, and through grave,
he calls you by name like each
and every luminary fixed
and every attending cherub.

A SOLSTICE POEM

(Marquette, MI at dusk)

Lights. Snow. Bright moon.
Visible Venus and crisp air.
Marquette. The Ore Dock.
The sun has fallen asleep;
the clamor subsides and
I am fully awake in the dusky
dying of the year. Solstice.
Winter. Arrival. Come heaven,
to this frozen shoreline town,
to these dimming days unlit.

THE TRAIN
OF HIS ROBE

...is filled with the glory of all the stars

Light gathers
to you Yahweh,
like fireflies to
a field on a soft-pink summer evening,
shimmer-brimming and flickerous.
Magnitude and radiance,
immeasurable in you.
Brightness adorns you,
luminosity encircles your
head like a star-crusted crown
and I bow,
an astronaut prophet,
a voyager and vagabond
through the far-reaches
of deep heaven.

This too, is your temple...
and I tread in craft
and sealed suit,
on holy ground.

WRECKAGE/SALVAGE

Star debris zipped hot
and eye-bogglingly fast,
cutting like little blowtorching bullets
through tortanium hull.
And there went B-Wing,
severed, lanced like a bulbous boil.
An observation deck no more.
The self-inflating foam filled in
the gaping wound and two humans
were sent bouncing through nothing
liked a popped eyeball with red,
unsocketed wires falling out the back.

There was no blood, just a fast-action
cauterization in silent horror.
Two seconds is all it took to make
this part of the ship a deserted island of
wreckage and slippage through
swallowing space.

And the clock started ticking.
And the air was measured.
There was a little bit of food.

Oh the curse'd calculus.
Oh how rudimentary and rude
were the few rations, oblivious
to their recent uptick in value.

The two humans—
a husband, a wife—shook in shock,
torn before, but never like this.
They saw their collective 82 years
in one another's reel-to-real reflections.
Streaming tears fluttered to droplets,
which would eventually need to be drunk.
No plans could find form.
Their hands warmed to a touch
before emergency gloves were found.
Their collective breath formed
a wordless word bubble around them....

The pain of needed salvage
was more tearing than any
ripping rock could rend.

THE TELESCOPE MAN

The Telescope Man climbed the last rungs of his very long ladder, to fit his last mirror in place. This looking glass was the size of a skyscraper, on its side of course, slightly upturned. He had mounted it on his own house, many years before, when it was but a fraction of the size, and had spent year after year adding section after jury-rigged section, improving its range. He was known by all to have kept saying, "I just want to look God in the eye."

And so, the Telescope Man built his life's work, a behemoth of metal and gears, mirrors and settings. He spent all he had. It took all his time. The neighbors, like Noah's must have, thought him crazy and called him worse. His wife and kids shook their heads, yet never left. Holding on to hope, they even helped from time to time. Albeit, obsession had almost stolen everything from him. He was dead-set: to pierce atmosphere and cloud, exosphere and nebula, to see to the backboard of the universe, to look God in the eye.

With the help of his mighty load-lifter, "The Looker-

Helper" he called it (for he wasn't so great with names), he went about the fastening and focusing of the last of the great mirrors to peer into empyrean. His kin continued to look on with a faint hope that his quest was almost realized, his mental thirst nearly slaked.

Then, unannounced and uninvited, a prophet knocked at the observatory door.

He bid gently to come and see. He spoke kindly to the Telescope Man's patient wife: "I would very much like to speak with your husband...and look at what he has made." She, scatter-mindedly, obliged and let him into their home-turned-giant-telscope-base. She detected no treachery, no despising. Simple curiosity and peaceful poise marked the plain-clothed prophet's demeanor. With a directional nod at the first of many staircases, he motioned that he would head up and see what the Telescope Man was up to. The wife returned a slow, affirming glance.

Step-by-step, first regular, interior staircases and then an attic staircase and then shingled makeshift...and then metal steps and ladders, the prophet climbed steadily and silently to meet the Telescope Man and his final work of looking into the outer reaches.

The prophet continued. Through thinner air and colder temperatures, he kept stepping up and up. Through starry curtain, he made his final approach. No light pollution now, nothing disturbed the view of dark, crisp space and the many suns and worlds hanging within.

The Telescope Man had heard the prophet approaching but paid little mind and didn't even turn to look. He was just riveting the last few rivets as the Looker-Helper mech was letting go of the last of the staggeringly expensive, humongous mirrors when the prophet reached the final platform. "There," he heard him say, "That oughta do it." The Telescope Man sighed a long and mostly-satisfied sigh, only half turning to the prophet in acknowledgement of his presence before he began his focusing.

"I suppose you want to see what all the fuss is about like all the others," the Telescope Man industriously and triumphantly snapped.

"Well, yes, in a way...that's right," the prophet measuredly responded.

"Today, my good sir, I am going to look God in the eye! This telescope, with its properly pointed mirrors and clockwork gears, is finally finished and aligned. This time I'm sure of it!"

The Telescope Man turned a bit more to shoot a glance of pride and surety at the prophet.

"Is that so?" queried the prophet. "That IS what I've heard you are doing...please...don't let me slow you down or get in your way. I'm merely here to observe."

The Telescope Man made no response, but paused for a couple seconds, turning a bit more to look at the prophet. His assessment was the same as his wife's had been when the prophet had first entered the house down below. No harm was in his face, no thrown shame fixed in his kind look. The Telescope Man quickly set and checked the last of the rivets using all his wits not to get in a hurry, for he was giddy and ecstatic at finishing his life's work. The day had come. The hour was upon him. He would now look through the largest, most powerful telescope ever constructed by man, and he would finally look God in his eye!

Instead of walking down the 30-runged, last ladder, he grabbed the side rails and slid down like a trained acrobat. The Telescope Man then remotely calibrated his colossal looking device and brought the viewfinder to his eye, one elongated and shaped just for his height and his eye. He focused, stepped back a couple times, and refocused. The further galaxies, quasars, and black-hole wonders darted through his circular view. Things never before seen, but they did not impress him. He shuffled his feet, recalibrated again, repositioned the eyepiece, sweated, then muttered.

He did this several times, each less measured and careful than the previous attempt. And with each, the prophet took one ladder step down, closer... and closer...and closer...til he was one step behind the frantic Telescope Man.

"I don't understand," he mouthed exasperatedly.

"By all the calculations and from all the data and theories of the best astronomers...I should have been able to see right into God's eye...I should have been able to look right at him!"

The prophet inched a bit closer and put a comforting, reassuring hand on the trembling Telescope Man's shoulder. "And you did...you did look into his eye. You can actually stare straight into it without this giant looking-glass."

The Telescope Man looked at him as if he were a gentle lunatic, while simultaneously allowing the prophet to back him up from the viewfinder, take his shoulders and square him forward and upward at the dome of constellations seen from the platform on which they stood.

"Oh man of toil and time busily spent, the whole thing is his eye...every star...every galaxy, all the colorful nebula bright and blazing...these are but flecks in the iris. Don't you see? Take another look...." At this the prophet shot his wonder and gaze into deep heaven, as the Telescope Man surveyed his countenance and caught a shooting star in the glassy reflection of pupil and lens.

"Breathe. Adjust your eyes to that of a child's, my dear looker, and do not be dismayed, your estimation of the sheer size of the eye was simply too small."

THE JAMES WEBB TELESCOPE

We just threw a 10 Billion-dollar looking glass
into orbit almost 900,000 miles into space.
It rode the back of a rocket to escape the Earth,
jettisoned, and unfurled.
Loaded with infrared tech and imaging prowess,
seeing tools and heat shields...
this mirrored time machine will
attempt to look back
to where everything
first exploded.

Inevitably, like a cosmic cartoon,
I hope they find you, full of pomp and
expanse, with one hilariously huge hand
resting on the exploder,
grinning.

JA-PETTO 7000

After giving it a man's lifetime of thought,
he took to his main shoulder pivots and
socket with one-handed precision.
The motorized wrench backed out the
alloyed socket bolts quickly,
as he felt a part of himself
loosen and go limp.
His right hand deadened in circuit and
synapse. The fingers fell.
He felt feeling no more,
the loss then held in his one,
working hand.

With great care, the metal man removed
his whole arm with a grunt and long breath,
as one might uproot a young tree too soon,
primed to fruit.
Without skipping another gyroscopic heartbeat,
he began dissecting the rods and servos,
the pistons and the rings.
The former bicep beams would make
for small legs,
the gearing for joints,

two elbow rings for socketed eyes.
Out of his old fingers he made
two small sets of fingers,
out of the running forearm cylinders,
a rib cage and a spine.

Hours turned into days.
His workmanship took more and more shape,
finally fitted with a face,
and a small strut and nut for a nose.
Power was then mainlined into the little frame
straight from a cable via four-prong-plug
into the spinning, made heart
within his chest plates.
Small digits wiggled. The neck swiveled
ever so slightly.
The digital blue-lit eyes locked
into his own green LEDs.

Before him sat new robotic life
of his own design,
a piecing of his pieces, rod of his rods,
a son of his right arm.

-400°

This must be what it is like
on one of those outer ice ball
planets orbiting in the near-dark,
absolutely chilling to the core,
at -400° or some lower,
voided temperature to human
minds. But if this numbed sphere
had a conscience, would
its slow, barely-moving thoughts
rest on a day, long-since
history, where warm
world-spinning hands
fashioned a frozen, dim
thing to rest in hibernation,
awaiting the bright, cresting
dawn of the promise
that all old stars will
be embraced and remember
their names?

LONE SENTRY

Ice bullets and -50°.
I now avert my eyes
from pure-driven beauty
and turn to survival.

The windchill slows the
antifreeze in the brain.
Chips malfunction. Interior
movements succumb
to slowness and fog.

Body shields up,
a shell really.
All power diverted
to primary systems.

This severity, systemic.
This bitter freezing, seeps.
If I had blood, I would be
dead...like I used to be.

Stasis.
Low power.
Sleep.

An iron pod,
folded up.
Surrounds.

Not...like...
I...used to...be...

Not dead. No....

GEMSTONE THOUGHTS

You have thoughts of me
so vast, broad do they expand,
numbered as the number
of minuscule grains of sand
and every...specific...particle...
particular. Every one.
They are precious, you say,
precious.

Uncountable in amount,
unweighable in worth
these are gemstones,
not merely thoughts
you think of me.
These are tiny, piled stars
for intricacy...
all the things you make of me,
too many to parse,
atoms to split,
and atoms DO.

Cerebral nuclear meltdown.

*see Psalm 139, esp. v. 6 & 17

I WAS SO YOUNG YESTERDAY

"I was so young yesterday," said the Green Lady.

I too, with her, have grown
old in a day, older still in two.
An age has passed inside my
body while the Earth rotated
merely 48 hours. What was
my name on Thursday? How
did children refer to this wizard's
legend last week? It is but a fading,
ancestor's memory, a flitting dimness
where a brilliant star once hung.

Who was I before? And how did I
exist is such ignorance when
brain and heart pulsed like an
infant's? Surely knowledge, and
that accepted humbly, does age
a woman, a man, in nonquantifiable
ways. And mysterious internal gearings
of change break all barriers of time,
kissing the edges of the eternal.

*The Green Lady, from C.S. Lewis' *Perelandra*

THE DRAGON
& HIS MOONS

Like Io and Europa,
stealing past the gas giant dragon
with gaping red eye,
swirling fury and cloud,
enfogging angry smoke
from colossal nostril.
A hardly-slumbering storm
of a world, swells like lungs.
So...slowly...they...creep,
sentry satellites, submissive.
Frightful witnesses in orbital slink.
Churning, you can see Jupiter
breathing to reach
and swallow these
sneaking moons
whole.

THE LAST

And there he was, last of the Scrawlers on his sphere, last of anyone on that planet. His emerald pen—glass tipped—dropping from his hand, one of two tools wielded by his ilk. His other hand tight-fistedly clutched the last of the sacred scrolls from the mind of the Spitter, former thoughts carried to him by vision and wing: these were the Sterngeist, ghosts of ancient stars. He had always done all he could to record every word, in meditation and calm, knowing that someone, somewhere may read this and know what may be coming. The burning terra firma. The hollowed bodies. The infilling dark.

Like bottles...like bottles they fell. Sucked out, unfilled. Vacated. Emptied. Yet refilled, not with nothing, but something worse. A vacuum. A recurring implosion of light and atmosphere. It fell in upon itself. It was absence, the outline of body, but the black hole of netherspace closely contained in shape. A formed formlessness.

The Shadow Caste had fallen on his world. They

came in blotting barrage. They swept in from the heavens to bring their own hollowing hell. Fast. Swarming. Bent. Life—they siphoned and sucked it. They ate the living light like a meat. That's right, to spite all that is glory-filled and pure, they ate the light. They trampled villages and homes. They even burnt the oldest of the temples and shredded the scrolls with slicing air. The rampant ones. The carnivorous cads. These plowers of worlds, and treaders of heads.

"Spitter help us all...El Owr...the Broadcaster of the Array...One from Elsewhere, acting Elseways... where are you...we have fallen prey to vile claws and given up ghost to a devouring darkness." Jehô had prayed and prayed out loud til his voice gave way to rasp, til "all" was only him, in the last days leading up to his evacuation. He had cried out and pleaded. His brethren, his guild of Etchers and Scrawlers, had fallen on all other fronts til he alone —alone—lonely and tremble-wracked, stood and wrote as he petitioned. Parchment scratched by jeweled, calligrapher's nib. Skins stained leaf-ink green, filling the character cuts, viridescent from penmark.

Even as the last moment of visitation had come from Lurgan, Lord of Far-worlds, Watcher of Spaces & Moons, Rider of Comet-tails, all slowed and sped erratic in polar shift after polar shift. The last chapter chronicling this obliterating bust-up, finality, and prophecy was to be scrawled on parchment with pen of emerald, with point of hardened glass. The Scrawler staggered and swayed like a spiritless man. When glass nibs were used, brightness emitted from the demarcation, solely illumined by pure fractured sunlight. This pen-dagger. This tool. This blade. This last stand. Did it even matter in the tidal storm of such swarming villainy? All faith and hope had nearly vanished from recall as the sweeping Caste bore down.

Yet, there was protection. Light shone to combat. Lurgan and his sisters, She-wings holy, fueled by fury and valiance, warding with splayed feather-plate and shielding sail. Peering back, over-shoulder, armored from eternities past, glinting with striking eye and unwavering duty.

"Scrawler! Etcher of metal and skins taut and tanned! Use what is in your hands! Write these words Jehô son of Ida, last of these dying lands... to warn the other worlds yet unconsumed in the path of the Caste. You must complete the Scroll lit by deep-green pen, in the hand of hope. You do have the aged ink of the Trunklord Cedarian, do you not?! I promise you small one, El Owr means to fortify and rebuild the things that have been destroyed and restore the light that has been stolen. As soon as the Sun be melded once more, the Broken One fused in heart, for a time it is given away and He lies asleep in self-effected weakness— he WOULD do such a thing as this. Even we Sterngeist know not why...fully, except...we know him to be good. Come Jehô, let us finish with these words...."

Lurgan and his war band fended and fended, hour-long, to spare the scrawler one last shred of time to finish what the verdurous ink to future peoples must tell.

Jehô both relaxed and mounted courage respectively. For the moment, his feet still tasted solid firmament, readied. He had just enough rolled tuskus* skin slung across his back. He removed his gemstalk pen dagger for the very last time, then uncorked the cork on his most matchless well of ink. The blood of Cedarian still had a faint glow and voice, for it had cost him much to gift it to Jehô long ago. There was no deep trance, no driven force, just hot clarity activating all his gifts at once. As consecrated conduit, words pierced his whole being from the farthest heavens. All shadow and dark-spun mischief swirled and thundered about him; all his land and the sphaera containing his land crumbled to space debris. With every sinew in hand and firing synapse in brain—he wrote, with eternity behind his eyes.

"With breaking he broke,
light from rupture,
love from bursted heart...
arc upon arc,
wave upon wave
shot through the Great Cloud of old.
He did not self-contain, though he could have.
What was in his mind for all the spat creation,
shards did fly, shards did leap,
hearts to mend, quadrillions to fix,
light erupted to the sphaerae held dear.
Each soulish creature to restore,
each shadow to vex with unapproachable light.

Darkness! Yes Darkness,
swallowed, consumed, digested for infinity.
By the magnitude, the superfluidity,
the awful, awful goodness!!!
Blessed be Lumanarius! Painter of Sound!
Bard of the Dawn!
For he alone is the Spitter's voice and song,
he alone can unsteal all that dark thieves
horde for themselves on charred and shattered
worlds.
And he alone …"

The prophet had had these lines cut through him like starfire to paper, beaming, heat-shot words, leaving emerald smoke to wisp from the skin, smelling faint and spicy sweet, like the day all locutions lept forth, when mouthed sounds were birthed. His faithful fingers had performed with unction, nearly possessed. Truth in purest form, delightsome to behold. And all the whole of the words were then sealed with molten wax from unseen hand. Ancient signet pressed, forever these lines would echo in space and time.

So Lurgan then touched Jehô Ida on the forefront of his illustrated head, master scrawler, and temple prophet of the Thurmm and Uhm,* former handler of sacred blades and preacher of the Light. Peace and perfections invaded the frazzled face. Phrases and poetries began to stream into his conscious and illumine visibly the complicated, collapsing atmosphere around him. Fingers animated and characters flowed, writing praises and lament semi-lucid. As all around, the schismatic scenery was turning over in earthy waves, dust, and floating rock, sounding like quake after cataclysmic quake and the undoing of his home sphaera. Collapse was imminent. Plates were folded. Geology was currently unlearning itself. Yet, on Jehô etched in the air; he wrote and wrote. Obviously, the latter apocalypse of Jehô Ida, Scrawler of the first aeon, had found no physical medium for root or purchase. Why some works find form and scanning eye and others do not, only the Spitter knows.

When the writings were writ, his world no longer bore light—it was utterly unmade. Later legends confessed that only the skyriders and patrolling Sterngeist caught a few lines and words dissipating into the nether spaces, for a couple centuries, finally passing out of known existence or legibility.

These were the last minutes of the Benten System and Benten 3 to be specific. Jehô, finishing the last characters, was encased in lit wing and shield, fortified by the mighty Lurgan, Captain of Early Creation. He was holding the penman up. He was now suspending him aloft. For, unbeknownst to Jehô, in messaging bliss, the last flatness of all the walkable world had given way beneath him.

The last day had lasted just this long.

Both body and scroll were now transported by the arms of one of the angels of space, carried beyond the Caste, beyond the dark, through star tunnel and trail, traversing other-realm and too many lightyears to fathom. In a space of time untold, to a new world he was brought, laid again on land, and cared for. And on this virgin sphere, the scrawler rested many days, his pen dagger at his side, his ancient inkwell upended, spilling the very last of its contents onto the newfound ground. He was borne by a Sterngeist, known through the ages as Glideran, a holy star remnant, suns of other systems and sentries of galaxies strewn through the universe.

The land—a substance he thought never to know again—which now held him word-drained and depleted, belonged to sphaera Tolerantia, "the place of patience," in the Arc of Nine, heretofore uninhabited. The last, this Jehô, had become the first.

*The Tuskus: a large, tusk-heavy land mammal of thick skin.

*Thurmm & Uhm: ancient sacred artifacts used by priests & prophets.

*LOCATION: Benten 3 of the enshadowed Benten System in the Starspitter Universe.
From the First Aeon, exact ancient date unknown.

FROZEN FOR STARS

This evening, I caught
my 14-year-old daughter
l i n g e r i n g
with neck bent,
looking long at
the winking skylights.
Awe-deaf, she didn't
hear me inquire
a second time
before I saw her gaze.
I froze with her at 10°
but not from the cold.
I tarried at the
shimmering worth,
warmed by the wondrous.
Oh daughter,
I know those stars
will always replay the
reminder of majesty beyond
this pain-shaken planet.

MY STAR-PRICKED HEART

I can't find the stars right now, Lord.
Maybe it's because the sun is up
and out, and pompous. Oh my
Starspitter, stuff my head full of
constellations; wrap me
in the color-soft capture of nebulae.
Bring me back to the big, holy, lostness...
to be found and then flourish
in hard light speckling the strong
night-veil. Remind me of the capacious
calculus that crafthanded the cosmos.

Oh my star-pricked heart,
breathe them in.
IMPRINT
the very next chance you get.

IN FRONT OF THE YOU

And so I weep, at those luminaries,
stellar sunlings and their burning works.
Tears and welling head, heavy,
made unready...for the great, gaping,
grandeur of the Galaxy-God, best
and bounding beyond the furthest
I have seen, that any of us have seen...
and here I sit again—whelmed, over
to be sure, discomfited by wrath-weight
meeting comfort-counterweight,
stretched, both towards an aching brain
and a peace that lays me down to sleep.
I'm throwing words into the
non-void knowing you are above,
further back as backdrop, over-lording
anti-listless, lively, lasting.
A world of names behind the name God,
good and glory-gorged,
swelling of might. I'm fighting
back the harbinging, heaven-bent song
sung in heldentenor, painting praise
with a heroic hue.

And this is all in front of the You. For,
"eye has not seen, ear has not heard"

VAPORIZED TOGETHER

...for Grace

I love you like the first two colonists
to miss the last star shuttle off a paydirt moon,
right before it was split clean and cleaved,
shattered by their sun's early supernova.
I, the suited man removing my helmet
to lean my sweaty forehead into yours,
to stop the fireball meteor shower,
in all its spectrum grandeur and gold,
from mirroring off your tigergreen eyes,
so I could see those known,
marbled orbs of invitation
like temples of sanctuary glass.
You, braids of velvet, tear-washed,
and smiling like a solar flare.
One breath...and two.
We lock. We die.
Vaporized into the heavens—together.

THE SUNCRAFTER'S COTTAGE

(PART 1) BROAD STROKE MELODY

Just where is your Suncrafter's workshop? And how can it contain the immense ingredients of star parts with liquids, matter, and gasses? Holily, they are held like pureswirl potions in colossal bottles. Where are these massive shelves to hold them? What über-ancient, gnarled, Trunklordish wood—smoothed in grain and goodliness—rests undergirding?

There must be a workbench of firststone fixed. Chairs of asteroidal rock, unfallen. A many-voiced wall of falling cataract on one side. A smelter's fire here also abides, white and blue, superheated in a cavelike hearth for igniting suns and flinging light through dark sky. And on another table, there is fur and horn and flex organic metals. Bone. Tooth. Claw. Beak. Sinew in jar. Skin in dish. Angelish wings hanging gossamer, translucent on angled hooks, older than any hook ever conceived by any hooked, human head.

How monolithic is this modest structure to house them? Proto-Alchemist of the Cosmos...how could this be? Where could this be?

Here, the spirits and souls come from within the Starspeaker, the Sower of Galaxies, the Suncrafter, the Spitter of Stars himself! A door opens into his chest where unspeakable, unthinkable, uneyeable and undeniable light is kept—brightstrong and brimming. These are heavenly doors, lifted up, heaved outward, givingly.

There is part of a roof overhead, but there is also direct access to the dauntless deeps, the heavens above and beyond. A place to release the stars to swim and the comets to streak. Space is not a vacuum of non-entity; it is an ocean of teeming, swimming worlds in orbit, swelling from the touch of the Crafter's hearty hands.

As each translucent orb of other-glass takes shape in magical grasp, a beard-wreathed smile is seen through the windowed transparency. Breath for atmosphere is inserted first, followed by rock, fire, water, gemstone, grass and animal. He is populating the globes, enormous, but palm-sized to him. Tinier gasses for breathability are injected with ancient, cylindrical syringe into these living worlds.

Yet there are some glass balls filled with elemental composite and winds, storm and dust, merely for beauty and the glint in the Spacebreather's eye. These sphaerae sometimes keep other living and bustling worlds alive by absorbing floating and racing space junk. There is great purpose even where there is no life.

All the blows, bustles, wheeling, reeling, or hustles heavenward, come from this "Maker's Place," the most ultra-epic of creative catacombs beyond the bounding beyond, larger than all life. THIS is the Suncrafter's cottage.

(PART 2) FINE STROKE HARMONY

Reveal to me your lordship of the stars,
how you shape them with
Potter's hands and spin them into their
far places with a painter's color-wetted brush,
spit in the mud...
mix, spin concoction...
and breathe out the
atmospheres of 50,000 worlds,
in multiplicity. Erupt! Release
light like a hot, overarching chorus!
How is it, Lord, that you lasso comets?
How is it, that you know the mass
of every black hole and speak through
them Vox Nebula?
I know not another who can put a hook in the
jaw of stars shooting or cast a net over
an entire meteor shower.
Truly your hands are too big for me to wholly
know.

Where were you when I established the Earth?
Tell me, if you have understanding.

Who fixed its dimensions? Certainly you know!
Who stretched a measuring line across it?

What supports its foundations?
Or who laid its cornerstone

while the morning stars sang together
and all the sons of God shouted for joy?

–JOB 38:4-7

THANKS & ACKNOWLEDGEMENTS

Emily Barnett>>>

For general generosity and fostering the Flash Fiction Magic community. You are mighty, a giant in the field of writing...and I'm just so happy to have met a best-seller BEFORE she made it big. Also, thank you for the name for my next book!

Andrea Renae>>>

For formatting & friendship, thank you. You paved the way with *Where Darkness Dwells* and your specific encouragement of this collection as possibly a work of worship gave me wings to fly to space again and again. You are quite amazing—KEEP GOING!

Proofreaders & Beta Readers>>>

Corey, BRR, Andrea, Vanessa, Rachael, Rachel, Randy, Cassie, Sarah, and anyone I may have forgotten! YOU ARE ALL WONDERFUL.

Jelly Helmet (Kelly Hellmuth)>>>

It's not everyday that you meet someone who you swear you already know, like REALLY know. Thank you, Kelly, for the honesty; brutal, ridiculous, and otherwise. Your empathy, tenacity, and holiness run deep through the Cottage, and I have greatly benefited from just knowing you. And you are ALWAYS up for reading, giving feedback, and helping edit.

K8 Stein>>>

All I can say, Kate, is that I know that you "see me." And to be seen in this mess of a world is something to be cherished. Thank you warmly for your throughly sci-fi heart, your love of space, and your excitement and enthrall for all things Star Wars. And I love that we both have ADHD...which is a weird thing to say, but I said it anyway.

To the Flash Fiction Magic Cottage>>>

There has never been a more wretched hive of fun and tomfoolery...typos, memes, audio messages, and gut-splittery™. You all are some of the wiliest and the best. Thank you 1.7 trillion times for the serious prayers and discussions, the inside jokes and acceptance, and the laughing that turns to real tears. Til we meet in real life or the very real writing cottage in the New Earth (I just love how "sci-fi" that sounds here), keep telling stories and building worlds. I'm gonna go watch Edge of Tomorrow in the basement! (that's right, Rachel)

Tristan Clark>>>
Thank you for being my closest friend in the Upper Peninsula and for your depth, laughter, and willingness to love imagination, D&D, card games, and fantasy and sci-fi movies. Your spirit-filled cooking, meat-smokery, and kindness have been a great comfort to me in the darkest seasons of my life. May you be richly blessed by the Creator for being very present in the lives of many.

Jamin Still>>>
For art, depth, constant encouragement and blessing. Your pointers and support in professional "making" have been a huge catalyst in me making it this far (however far that is!). Thanks man. May many a Marco Polo be before us!

Kyra Hinton>>>
Thank you for being like a flesh & blood nerdy cousin, for fellowship deconstructing, for letting me cuss, and for owning a lightsaber. You have granted me so much insight into art and creativity and how to get things to work within that weird liminal space of selling what I create. Listen kid, now I owe YOU one!

Sarah Spradlin>>>

Sarah, thank you for "sistering" me, and feeling like blood, kin, and making everywhere we show up together feel like family. You are one incredible human, and your determination and straight-forwardness shine like many suns in their strength. You are ever-ready and always jumping at the chance to be present and bless. I cannot thank you enough for your friendship.

Pastor Randy Edwards>>>

Hey Randy, thanks not just for who you are, but for your honest-to-goodness voice (your actual reading voice), your sonnets, and your humility and humor. You SERIOUSLY bless my socks off! If I lived anywhere near you, I would be at your church every Sunday.

Every friend from The Rabbit Room
& Poetry Pub>>>

Thank you Jen & Chris Yokel, Chris Wheeler, etc. for what you started. The Poetry Pub has been a very rich, encouraging, safe, and incredible writing family of pro-caliber poets! Amelia, Charissa, Noelle, Amy, Sunny, Spencer, Pastor Ben Squires, and so many more. You all make me a better poet and human.

Marty Achatz>>>

I just have to say thank you, Marty, for being a huge supporter and friend in the local poetry and art community. Your heart for poetry and your great sense of humor are supremely encouraging, and I'm glad I know you. Bigfoot forever.

Troy Graham>>>

Who would have thought that the Great Wordhurler would bring Troy Graham back into my life to throw a few sparks on a tinderbox full of poetry yet to be written. But...you know what, he did, and I am so thankful for that, Troy, you have no idea.

B.G. Bradley>>>

Thanks for the books man! And the kindness...and comparing me to William Blake. You were like the third serious person to do that in a few months and I think it's gonna stick. To be compared to a cosmic maniac of poetry and visual art means a lot!

Jake Medlong>>>

For more late-night talk-athons than maybe anyone I've ever known. Also, for leather goods, authenticity, and one of the longest friendships I've ever, ever had.

Grace>>>

I think it was 2016, and we were traveling in the west pulling our camper and stopped to camp just outside of Moab, UT, down the Colorado River at like 9:00 in the evening. Once the kids were all in bed, I remember looking up and seeing a celestial display like I've never seen before, and we stayed up for like an hour just looking at it together and taking it all in. It was still. It was captivating. I just want to say I am so glad we shared that moment together—it was unforgettable...so are our many travels...and so is our love.

Hosanna, the Warcry>>>

Maybe unbeknownst to you, but it was you who sparked a deep flame of creativity in me many years ago as a little baby, writing songs and poems. I'm so thankful for your hard, hard work and your strength... and for watching weird sci-fi movies with me through the years, some of which sucked real bad. To you I dedicate the poem It Was Star Wars.

ZURI, our Rock>>>

For being the bright and imitable galaxy of personality that you are...and for being the superb inspiration for one of the best poems in this collection, IMO. Keep reading and painting Zuri!

Torah Despereaux Rose>>>

For being my buddy, my art market companion, an unbelievable example of friendliness and kindness, and a serious budding artist in your own right. Keep creating T!

Hallel, the Righteous Ember>>>

I am always impressed with you, Hallel. You are so imaginative, sweet, and thoughtful. I'm sure there are 100 things you could do in life, but part of me thinks there's a blossoming writer inside you.

Mom>>>

for showing me the beauty of art & music at a young age.

Dad>>>

for taking me to see *E.T.* & *Star Wars*.

Corey, Scott, Sean, & Steven from
Makers & Mystics>>>

Thanks for the constant invitation to be a part of something so cool. You guys really help me bless my "holy weirdness."

Doug McKelvey>>>

For so many Rabbits out there, it's Andrew Peterson (and I should thank him too), but for me, it's you. I'm indebted forever to your laser-accurate poetry and for Every Moment Holy in general. Your words have, in so many cases, given me mine.

Wendell Berry>>>

Oddly, Mr. Berry, you are the poet who probably makes more sense to me than anyone living or dead. Even more oddly, you have written darn near everything in a small, known space in Kentucky, and I write about things so far away it breaks my brain. But somehow, it works...and you have influenced me to no end. And anyway, Kentucky happens to be on a fast-spinning sphere in outer space, in the Milky Way galaxy, which makes us basically the same.

George Lucas>>>

C.S. Lewis had a different George (McDonald), and I have you and the sprawling universe you thought up. I'm sure neither you nor any members of the Jedi Council will ever read this, but just the same as C.S. said, "You baptized my imagination."

Rebecca E>>>
For always-thoughtful conversations and helping me with a discerning eye on my cover.

Sports Rack Family>>>
Thanks for making a place for me over six years ago and being a great bunch of people to work and play with.

LAST TRANSMISSION>>>>>>>>

"Our thoughts of you Lord have been too small, too few."

Let's change that.

End.

-Doug McKelvey, "A Liturgy of Praise to the King of Creation"
from *Every Moment Holy Vol. 1*